This book belongs to

....

(that's me!)

D0336267

For Jessie, my wee star – CC
Extra special thanks to Gussie – LDB

Published by Little Door Books 2020
This edition published in 2021

ISBN : 9781999955670

Text copyright Corrina Campbell 2020
Illustrations copyright Corrina Campbell 2020

The right of Corrina Campbell to be identified as author and illustrator of this work has been
asserted in accordance with the Copyright, Designs and Patents Act 1988. All rights reserved.
No part of this publication may be reproduced, stored in a retrieval system, or transmitted
in any form or by any means, electronic, mechanical, photocopying, recording or otherwise,
without prior permission of the publishers.
A CIP catalogue record for this book is available from the British Library.

Little Door Books and Little Door Debuts acknowledges support from the National
Lottery through Creative Scotland towards the publication of this title.

LOTTERY FUNDED

Email: mail@littledoorbooks.co.uk
Website: www.littledoorbooks.co.uk
Twitter: @littledoorbooks, @LDDebuts

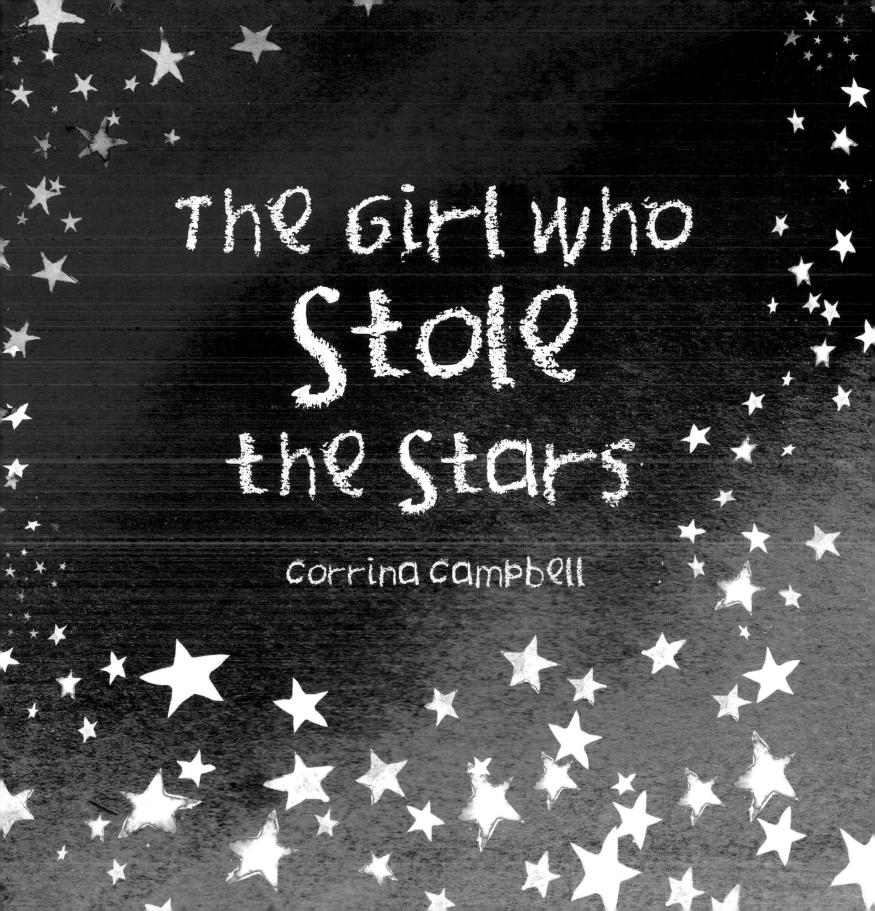

The Girl Who Stole the Stars

Corrina Campbell

Once there was a little girl Who
loved the **stars.**

All she Wanted Was to have a **star** of her very own.

Then she had an idea.

dear Santa,
please can I have
a ladder so that I
can reach the
stars.

Thank you.
+ + +

The present wasn't as big as she
had expected...

...but then this was
no ordinary present.

It Was exactly What
She had asked for...

...it Was a ladder to
the **stars.**

she climbed

up

and

up

and

up

The **stars** shone brightly in the night sky.
"No one will notice if I just take one,"
thought the little girl.

So she did.

The little girl loved her **star** but the **star** didn't seem happy.

I love you

It didn't shine as **brightly** as it had in the sky.

"Maybe my **star** just needs some friends?" thought the little girl.

So...

she climbed

up

and

up

and

up

there were HUNDREDS of stars in the sky.

"No one will notice if I just take a few more," thought the little girl.

so she did.

The little girl loved her stars but **still** the stars did not seem happy.

They were starting to lose their
sparkle.

"Maybe my **stars** just feel sad for the ones I left behind?"

thought the little girl.

So...

she climbed

UP

and

UP

and

UP

There were only a few **stars** left in the sky.

"No one will notice if I just take all of you,"

thought the little girl.

So she did.

NOW the little girl had **all** the
stars from the sky,

but the stars were getting

darker and darker and darker.

Then she remembered
the **moon.**
"Maybe my
stars need
a moon?"
thought the
little girl.

So...

she climbed

up

and

up

and

up

A lone **moon** shone bright in the dark night sky.

"No one will notice if I just take the moon too," thought the little girl.

So she did.

NOW the little girl had **all** the stars **and** the moon.

She showed them how to **dance.**

She taught them how to **sing.**

But **still** the stars didn't seem happy.

However, it was christmas time and the little girl felt sure this would cheer them up.

Especially since Santa would be coming. Everybody loves Santa.

But What she didn't realise Was that

santa

wasn't

coming

because santa couldn't

see Where to go.

santa had always used the stars to guide him

and the moon to light the way

but now he was lost.

Then he remembered the little girl With the
magical ladder.

Perhaps she would know where
the **moon** and **stars** had gone?

He knocked on her window and the little girl appeared.
"I need your help," Santa exclaimed. "The moon and stars
are missing so I can't deliver the presents."

"Oh dear,"
said the little girl.
"I have them all here!"

"Don't worry...

...I'll put them back in
the sky for you right
away!"

So...

she climbed

up

and

up

and

up

"Goodbye stars," she shouted
as she scattered them across the sky.

"Thank you," called Santa as he flew **UP** and **UP** and **UP** into the night.

As the stars **sparkled** happily the little girl realised that the stars weren't actually hers to keep.

They were back in the night sky...

...for everyone to see.